FARMYARD FRIENDS

Gaston

the Goat

by Lisa Mullarkey
illustrated by Paula Franco

Calico Kid

An Imprint of Magic Wagon
abdopublishing.com

To vegetarians everywhere: Freckles, Gaston, Golden Girl and Daisy thank you! **—LM**

To Tina and Candice, for your hard work and patience! **—PF**

abdopublishing.com

Published by Magic Wagon, a division of ABDO, PO Box 398166, Minneapolis, Minnesota 55439. Copyright © 2018 by Abdo Consulting Group, Inc. International copyrights reserved in all countries. No part of this book may be reproduced in any form without written permission from the publisher. Calico Kid™ is a trademark and logo of Magic Wagon.

Printed in the United States of America, North Mankato, Minnesota.
052017
092017

Written by Lisa Mullarkey
Illustrated by Paula Franco
Edited by Megan M. Gunderson
Designed by Christina Doffing

Publisher's Cataloging-in-Publication Data

Names: Mullarkey, Lisa, author. | Franco, Paula, illustrator.
Title: Gaston the goat / by Lisa Mullarkey ; illustrated by Paula Franco.
Description: Minneapolis, MN : Magic Wagon, 2018. | Series: Farmyard friends
Summary: When a storm comes to Storm Cliff Stables, the camp lives up to its
    name, and Gaston the Goat fears he'll never get to sleep with all the rain,
    lightning, and thunder!
Identifiers: LCCN 2017930502 | ISBN 9781532140457 (lib. bdg.) |
    ISBN 9781624029929 (ebook) | ISBN 9781624029974 (Read-to-me ebook)
Subjects: LCSH: Goats--Juvenile fiction. | Friendship--Juvenile fiction. |
    Thunderstorms--Juvenile fiction.
Classification: DDC [Fic]--dc23
LC record available at http://lccn.loc.gov/2017930502

Table of Contents

Chapter 1
A Thunder Boom

The sun disappeared behind a cloud.

Poof!

The blue sky turned gray.

Piff!

The wind whistled.

Whoosh!

"Close the shutters," said Kianna.
She peered out the barn window.
"Mama says we're getting a thunder
boom."

A goat darted into the barn. It
rammed into Kianna.

"Hi, Gaston." Kianna giggled.
"What's wrong?"

"Bleat, bleat," said Gaston.

"The goats are afraid of the rain,"
said Aunt Jane.

"Don't be scared," said Kianna. "It's
just a little water."

"Bleat, bleat, bleat."

Aunt Jane glanced at the sky. "We're getting a storm, that's for sure." She scritch-scratched Gaston's neck. "Springtime is rain time at Storm Cliff Stables."

"BLEAT! BLEAT! BLEAT!"

Kianna hugged Gaston.

Flash went the lightning.

Crash went the thunder.

Down came the rain.

Down, down, down, down, down.

Aunt Jane said, "Let's go find your mama, Kianna."

They dashed out the door. They darted across the pasture. They left Gaston behind.

Chapter 2
Bleat! Bleat! Bleat!

"Stop your bleating," said Freckles.

Flashity-flash-flash!

"It's just a little lightning," Freckles said.

11

Crashity-crash-crash!

"And a little thunder," said Daisy.

Splashity-splash-splash!

"And a little rain," said Golden Girl.

Gaston shook. He shivered. His

lips quivered. "Bleat, bleat, bleat,

bleat, bleat! Then I will be just a little

scared."

But Gaston was not just a little scared. He was a lot scared. Too scared to play kick the can. Too scared to eat dinner. And worst of all, too scared to go to sleep, sleep, sleep as the rain came down, down, down.

Gaston rubbed his eyes. He yawned. "If the rain keeps coming down, down, down, then I will be up, up, up all night. BLEAT, BLEAT, BLEAT."

"Stop bleating," said Daisy.

"Sorry," said Gaston. "But I am tired and afraid. BLEAT!"

Golden Girl jumped up on Daisy's stool. Then she flew onto her nesting box. "It's only a little rain. Close your eyes. Go to sleep. When you wake up, the storm will be over."

"I cannot sleep. The storm is too scary for me," said Gaston. He paced back and forth and back and forth and back and forth again.

Golden Girl clucked. "I have an idea."

"Is it a good idea?" asked Gaston. "Will it make me forget about the storm?"

16

Golden Girl bobbed her head up and down. "It is a very good idea. Let's sing a song. Singing will make you forget about the rain."

Gaston's friends sang, "It's raining, it's pouring, the old farmer is . . ."

Gaston stomped his hoof. "Stop, stop, stop! That song will not help me forget about the rain. That song is about rain." He paced again. "BLEAT!"

The flashing got brighter. The crashing boomed louder. The rain came down harder.

"BLEAT! BLEAT! BLEAT!"

Golden Girl sighed. "My idea
was not a good idea. I will think of
another one."

Gaston yawned and paced again.
If the rain kept coming down, down,
down, how would he ever sleep,
sleep, sleep?

Chapter 3
Lots of Ideas

Freckles, Daisy, and Golden Girl wanted to help Gaston.

"You need to relax," said Freckles. "Take a mud bath. You will feel better."

"No, no, no," said Gaston. "I cannot go outside in the rain. It is too bright. Too loud. The lightning will flashity-flash-flash. The thunder will crashity-crash-crash! BLEAT!"

"Then moooove into the milk stand," said Daisy. "It is in the darkest part of the barn. It's quieter, too. You will feel safe. You can sleep there."

Gaston swished his ears forward. "That is a good idea!" He skittered into the milk stand. It was darker. It was quieter. He felt better until . . .

Flashity-flash-flash!

Crashity-crash-crash!

"BLEAT! BLEAT! BLEAT! It is not dark enough," said Gaston. "It is not quiet enough."

Golden Girl tipped Gaston's bucket of goat feed over. "Then put this bucket over your head. It will be much darker. Much quieter."

Gaston squirmed. Now it was too dark. And the bucket squish-squashed his ears. "This bucket is not a good idea."

Gaston shivered. His lips quivered. He yawned again. "Bleat, bleat, bleat. Since the rain is still coming down, down, down, will all of you stay up, up, up with me?"

Chapter 4
The Best Idea

Daisy yawned and nodded.

Golden Girl yawned and nodded.

Freckles yawned. Twice. But he did

not nod.

Flashity-flash-flash!

Crashity-crash-crash!

"BLEAT! BLEAT! BLEAT!"

"We need another idea," said
Freckles. "A better idea. If we don't
get one, then we will be up, up, up all
night."

Freckles looked to the left.

He looked to the right.

He spied Pip and Squeak asleep in their stalls. "I know what to do!"

Gaston didn't believe him. He groaned. He moaned.

"This is the best idea ever," said Freckles. "Just you wait and see."

Freckles trotted over to Pip and Squeak. He tug-tug-tugged at their blankets. He dragged them over to the milk stand. "We will make a tent for you."

With a tuck-tuck here and a tuck-tuck there, the tent was done.

"I cannot see the lightning," said Gaston. "I cannot hear the thunder. Thank you, thank you, thank you! This is the best idea ever!"

Daisy mooed and swished her tail.

Golden Girl clucked and flapped her wings.

Freckles snorted and rolled in the straw.

31

But a few minutes later . . .

Flashity-flash-flash!

Crashity-crash-crash!

Splashity-splash-splash!

The friends froze. They waited. But they did not hear bleat, bleat, bleat.

It was quiet in the tent until . . .

"Zzzzzzzzzzzzzzz . . ."